For D. A. Willis—*J. W.*

For Nelly—*T. R.*

Atheneum Books for Young Readers

An imprint of Simon & Schuster Children's Publishing Division

1230 Avenue of the Americas, New York, New York 10020

Text copyright © 2005 by Jeanne Willis

Illustrations copyright © 2005 by Tony Ross

First published in Great Britain in 2005 by Andersen Press Ltd.

The text for this book is set in Celeste.

The illustrations for this book are rendered in pastels.

Manufactured in Italy

First U. S. edition 2006

2 4 6 8 10 9 7 5 3 1

CIP data for this book is available from the Library of Congress.

ISBN-13: 978-1-4169-1490-7

ISBN-10: 1-4169-1490-0

Gorilla! Gorilla!

Jeanne Willis and Tony Ross

Atheneum Books for Young Readers
NEW YORK   LONDON   TORONTO   SYDNEY

A mother mouse's baby has gone missing.

She went up the mountain.

Down the mountain.

Round and round the rainforest.
But she still couldn't find him.
The rainforest was very, very big,
And the baby was very, very small.
The mouse thought she'd lost him forever.

Just when things
couldn't get any worse . . .

Out jumped a great, big, hairy, scary ape!
"Gorilla! Gorilla!" she squeaked.
"Help! Help! He'll catch me!
He'll squash me and scratch me,
He'll mince me and mash me,
And crunch me up for lunch!"

"Stop!"

bellowed the gorilla.

But the mouse ran and ran.
Over the bridge, over the sea,
All the way to China.
But the gorilla was never far behind.
"Who are you running from, Mouse?" asked Panda.
"A killer gorilla!" she squeaked,
"Help! Help! He'll catch me!
He'll squash me and scratch me,
He'll mince me and mash me,
And crunch me up for lunch!"

"Stop!" bellowed the gorilla,
But the mouse ran and ran.
All the way to America.

But the gorilla was catching up.

"Who are you running from, Mouse?" asked Chipmunk.
"A killer gorilla," she squeaked.
"Help! Help! He'll catch me!
He'll squash me and scratch me,
He'll mince me and mash me,
And crunch me up for lunch!"

"**Stop!**" bellowed the gorilla.

But the mouse ran and ran.

Into a submarine. Under the sea.
All the way to Australia.

The gorilla had almost caught up.

"Who are you
running from, Mouse?"
asked Koala.

"A killer gorilla!" she squeaked.
"Help! Help! He'll catch me!
He'll squash me and scratch me,
He'll mince me and mash me,
And crunch me up for lunch!"

"Stop!" bellowed the gorilla.
But the mouse ran and ran,
Across the desert. Into the submarine.
Under the sea. Across the ice.
All the way to the Arctic.
She looked around.

She was all alone . . .

Except for the gorilla!

"*Stop!*"

he bellowed.

The mouse tried to run, but she was too tired.
The snow was so thick, and she'd run
such a long way.
The gorilla came closer . . .

and closer . . .

And *closer!*

The mouse stood still. She shivered and shut her eyes.
She wished she could see her baby once more,
Before she was eaten.

"Here he is!" said the gorilla.

Cradled in his huge hands was the baby mouse.

"I found him in the forest," said the gorilla.
"I was trying to give him back, but you wouldn't stop!
Who were you running from, Mouse?"

The mouse looked into his kind, brown eyes
And blushed.
"Oh . . . nobody you know!" she squeaked.
"I'm not frightened now."

"Even so, it's a big, scary world
Out there," said the gorilla.
"Let me carry you home.
You'll feel much safer."

And the mouse did.

E
Willis

Willis, Jeanne.

Gorilla! Gorilla!

$15.95

DATE			